HORRiD HENRY'S Thank You Letter

Francesca Simon
Illustrated by Tony Ross

Orion
Children's Books

Horrid Henry's Thank You Letter originally appeared in
Horrid Henry's Underpants first published in Great Britain in 2003 by
Orion Children's Books
This edition first published in Great Britain in 2011
by Orion Children's Books
a division of the Orion Publishing Group Ltd
Orion House
5 Upper Saint Martin's Lane
London WC2H 9EA
An Hachette UK Company

The Orion Publishing Group's policy is to use papers that
are natural, renewable and recyclable products and made
from wood grown in sustainable forests. The logging and
manufacturing processes are expected to conform to the
environmental regulations of the country of origin.

A catalogue record for this book is available from the British Library.

Printed and bound in China

www.orionbooks.co.uk
www.horridhenry.co.uk

HORRiD HENRY'S
Thank You Letter

For Sabrina and Jordan Jade

Look out for . . .

Don't Be Horrid, Henry!
Horrid Henry's Birthday Party
Horrid Henry's Holiday
Horrid Henry's Underpants
Horrid Henry Gets Rich Quick
Horrid Henry and the Football Fiend
Horrid Henry's Nits
Horrid Henry and Moody Margaret

There are many more **Horrid Henry** books
available. For a complete list visit
www.horridhenry.co.uk
or
www.orionbooks.co.uk

Contents

Chapter 1

Ahh! This was the life!
A sofa, a telly, a bag of crisps.
Horrid Henry sighed happily.

"Henry!" shouted Mum from the kitchen. "Are you watching TV?"

Henry blocked his ears.
Nothing was going to interrupt
his new favourite TV programme,
Terminator Gladiator.

"Answer me, Henry!" shouted Mum. "Have you written your Christmas thank you letters?"

NO!

bellowed Henry.

Why not?

screamed Mum.

"Because I haven't," said Henry. "I'm busy." Couldn't she leave him alone for two seconds?

Mum marched into the room and switched off the TV.
"Hey!" said Henry. "I'm watching *Terminator Gladiator*."

"Too bad," said Mum. "I told you, no TV until you've written your thank you letters."

"It's not fair!" wailed Henry.

"I've written all *my* thank you letters," said Perfect Peter.

"Well done, Peter," said Mum.
"Thank goodness *one* of my children
has good manners."

Peter smiled modestly. "I always
write mine the moment I unwrap a
present. I'm a good boy, aren't I?"

"The best," said Mum.

"Oh, shut up, Peter," snarled Henry.

"Mum! Henry told me to shut up!"
said Peter.

"Stop being horrid, Henry. You will write to Aunt Ruby, Great-Aunt Greta and Grandma now."

"Now?" moaned Henry. "Can't I do it later?"

"When's later?" said Dad.

"Later!" said Henry. Why wouldn't they stop nagging him about those stupid letters?

Chapter 2

Horrid Henry hated writing
thank you letters.

Why should he waste his precious
time saying thank you for presents?
Time he could be spending
reading comics, or watching TV.

But no.

He would barely unwrap a present
before Mum started nagging.

She even expected him to write to
Great-Aunt Greta and thank her for
the Baby Poopie Pants doll.

Great-Aunt Greta for one did not
deserve a thank you letter.

This year Aunt Ruby had sent him
a hideous lime green cardigan.
Why should he thank her for that?

True, Grandma had given him £15,
which was great. But then Mum
had to spoil it by making him write
her a letter too.

Henry hated writing letters for nice presents every bit as much as he hated writing them for horrible ones.

"You have to write thank you letters," said Dad.

"But **why?**" said Henry.

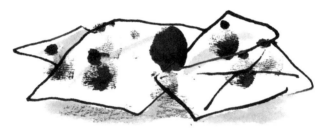

"Because it's polite," said Dad.

"Because people have spent time and money on you," said Mum.

So what? thought Horrid Henry.
Grown-ups had loads of time to do
whatever they wanted.

No one told them, stop watching
TV and write a thank you letter. Oh
no. They could do it whenever they
felt like it. Or not even do it at all.

And adults had tons of money compared to him. Why shouldn't they spend it buying him presents?

"All you have to do is write
one page," said Dad.
"What's the big deal?"

Henry stared at him. Did Dad have
no idea how long it would take him
to write one whole page?

Hours

and

 hours

 and

hours.

"You're the meanest, most horrible parents in the world and I hate you!" shrieked Horrid Henry.

"Go to your room, Henry!"
shouted Dad.

"And don't come down until
you've written those letters,"
shouted Mum. "I am sick and tired
of arguing about this."

Horrid Henry stomped upstairs.

Chapter 3

Well, no way was Henry writing
any thank you letters.

He'd rather **starve**.

He'd rather **die**.

He'd stay in his room for a month.

A year.

One day Mum and Dad would come
up to check on him and all they'd
find would be a few bones.
Then they'd be sorry.

Actually, knowing them, they'd probably just moan about the mess. And then Peter would be all happy because he'd get Henry's room and Henry's room was bigger.

Well, no way would he give them the satisfaction.

All right, thought Horrid Henry.
Dad said to write one page. In his
biggest, most gigantic handwriting,
Henry wrote:

DEAR AUNT
RUBY,
THANK YOU
FOR THE
PRESENT
HENRY

That certainly filled a whole page, thought Horrid Henry.

Mum came into the room. "Have you written your letters yet?"

"Yes," lied Henry.

Mum glanced over his shoulder. "Henry!" said Mum. "That is not a proper thank you letter."

"Yes it is," snarled Henry. "Dad said I had to write one page so I wrote one page."

"Write five sentences," said Mum.

Five sentences?

Five whole sentences?

It was completely impossible
for anyone to write so much.
His hand would fall off.

"That's way too much,"
wailed Henry.

"No TV until you write your letters," said Mum, leaving the room.

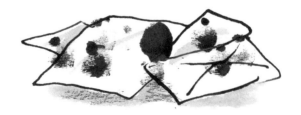

Chapter 4

Horrid Henry stuck out his tongue.
He had the meanest, most horrible
parents in the world.

When he was king any parent who even whispered the words 'thank you letter' would get fed to the crocodiles.

They wanted five sentences? He'd give them five sentences.

Henry picked up his pencil
and scrawled:

Dear Aunt Ruby,
No thank you for the
horrible present. It is
the worst present I have
ever had.

Anyway, didn't some old
Roman say it was better to
give than to receive? So in
fact, you should be writing
me a thank you letter.
Henry
P.S. Next time just
send money.

There! Five whole sentences.
Perfect, thought Horrid Henry.

Mum said he had to write a five
sentence thank you letter. She never
said it had to be a *nice* thank you
letter. Suddenly Henry felt quite
cheerful.

He folded the letter and popped
it in the stamped envelope Mum
had given him.

One down. Two to go.

In fact, Aunt Ruby's no thank you
letter would do just fine for
Great-Aunt Greta.
He'd just substitute
Great-Aunt Greta's name for
Aunt Ruby's and copy the rest.

Bingo. Another letter was done.

Now Grandma. She *had* sent money so he'd have to write something nice.

Thank you for the money, blah, blah, blah, best present I've ever received, blah, blah, blah, next year send more money, £15 isn't very much, Ralph got £20 from his grandma, blah, blah, blah.

What a waste, thought Horrid Henry
as he signed it and put it in the
envelope, to spend so much time
on a letter, only to have to write
the same old thing all over again
next year.

And then suddenly
Horrid Henry had a wonderful,
spectacular idea.

Why had he never thought of
this before?

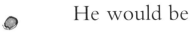

He would be

rich,

rich,

rich.

"There goes money-bags Henry," kids would whisper enviously, as he swaggered down the street followed by Peter lugging a hundred DVDs for Henry to watch in his mansion on one of his twenty-eight giant TVs.

Mum and Dad and Peter would be
living in their hovel somewhere,
and if they were very, very nice
to him Henry *might* let them watch
one of his smaller TVs for fifteen
minutes or so once a month.

Henry was going to start a business.
A business guaranteed to make
him rich.

Chapter 5

"Step right up, step right up,"
said Horrid Henry.

He was wearing a sign saying:

HENRY's Thank you letters
personal letters written
Just for you

A small crowd of children
gathered round him.

"I'll write all your thank you letters
for you," said Henry. "All you
have to do is to give me a stamped,
addressed envelope and tell me what
present you got. I'll do the rest."

"How much for a thank you letter?" asked Kung-Fu Kate.

"£1," said Henry.

"No way," said Greedy Graham.

"99p," said Henry.

"Forget it," said Lazy Linda.

"OK, 50p," said Henry.
"And two for 75p."

"Done," said Linda.

Henry opened his notebook.
"And what were the presents?"
he asked.

Linda made a face.
"Handkerchiefs," she spat.
"And a bookmark."

"I can do a 'no thank you' letter,"
said Henry.
"I'm very good at those."

Linda considered.

"Tempting," she said, "but then
mean Uncle John won't send
something better next time."

Business was brisk.
Dave bought three. Ralph bought
four 'no thank you's'.
Even Moody Margaret bought one.

Whoopee, thought Horrid Henry.

His pockets were jingle-jangling
with cash.

Now all he had to do was write seventeen letters. Henry tried not to think about that.

Chapter 6

The moment he got home
from school Henry went
straight to his room.
Right, to work, thought Henry.

His heart sank as he looked at the
blank pages. All those letters!
He would be here for weeks.
Why had he ever set up a
letter-writing business?

But then Horrid Henry thought.

True, he'd promised a personal letter
but how would Linda's aunt ever
find out that Margaret's granny had
received the same one?
She wouldn't!

If he used the computer, it would be a cinch. And it would be a letter sent personally, thought Henry, because I am a person and I will personally print it out and send it.

All he'd have to do was to write the names at the top and to sign them.

Easy-peasy lemon squeezy.

Then again, all that signing. And writing all those names at the top. And separating the thank you letters from the no thank you ones.

Maybe there was a better way.

Horrid Henry sat down at the computer and typed:

> Dear Sir or Madam,

That should cover everyone, thought Henry, and I won't have to write anyone's name.

> Thank you/No thank you
>
> for the
>
> a) wonderful
>
> b) horrible
>
> c) disgusting
>
> present.

I really loved/hated it.
In fact, it is the best present/worst
present I have ever received.
I played with it/broke it/ate it/spent it/
threw it in the bin straight away.
Next time just send lots of money.
Best wishes/ worst wishes,

 Now, how to sign it?
Aha, thought Henry.

Your friend
or relative.

Perfect, thought Horrid Henry.
Sir or Madam knows whether
they deserve a thank you
or a no thank you letter.
Let them do some work for a change
and tick the correct answers.

Print.

Print.

Print.

Out spewed seventeen letters.

It only took a moment to stuff
the letters in the envelopes.
He'd pop them in the postbox
on the way to school.
Had an easier way to become a
millionaire ever been invented?
thought Horrid Henry, as he turned
on the telly.

Ding dong.

It was two weeks after Henry set up
'Henry's Thank You Letters'.
Horrid Henry opened the door.
A group of Henry's customers
stood there, waving pieces of paper
and shouting.

"My granny sent the letter back and now I can't watch TV for a week," wailed Moody Margaret.

"I'm grounded!"
screamed Aerobic Al.

"I have to go swimming!"
screamed Lazy Linda.

"No sweets!"
yelped Greedy Graham.

"No pocket money!"
screamed Rude Ralph.

"And it's all your fault!"
they shouted.

Horrid Henry glared at his angry
customers. He was outraged.
After all his hard work, *this* was
the thanks he got?

"Too bad!" said Horrid Henry as he
slammed the door. Honestly, there
was no pleasing some people.

"Henry," said Mum.
"I just had the strangest phone call
from Aunt Ruby…"